Wild About Wheels

SNOWPLOWS

by Nancy Dickmann

PEBBLE
a capstone imprint

Pebble Emerge is published by Pebble, an imprint of Capstone.
1710 Roe Crest Drive
North Mankato, Minnesota 56003
www.capstonepub.com

Copyright © 2022 by Capstone. All rights reserved. No part of this publication may be reproduced in whole or in part, or stored in a retrieval system, or transmitted in any form or by any means, electronic, mechanical, photocopying, recording, or otherwise, without written permission of the publisher.

Library of Congress Cataloging-in-Publication Data
Names: Dickmann, Nancy, author.
Title: Snowplows / Nancy Dickmann.
Description: North Mankato, Minnesota : Pebble, [2022] | Series: Wild about wheels | Includes bibliographical references and index. | Audience: Ages 6-8. | Audience: Grades 2-3. | Summary: "Describes snowplows, including their main parts and how they keep roads safe to drive on"-- Provided by publisher.
Identifiers: LCCN 2020024145 (print) | LCCN 2020024146 (ebook) | ISBN 9781977132376 (library binding) | ISBN 9781977133311 (paperback) | ISBN 9781977154903 (ebook pdf)
Subjects: LCSH: Snowplows--Juvenile literature. | Snow removal--Juvenile literature.
Classification: LCC TD868 .D53 2022 (print) | LCC TD868 (ebook) | DDC 625.7/63--dc23
LC record available at https://lccn.loc.gov/2020024145
LC ebook record available at https://lccn.loc.gov/2020024146

Image Credits
Alamy: Chuck Eckert, 18–19; Getty Images: Davin G Photography, 12, Portland Press Herald, 8; iStockphoto: benoitb, 13, hansslegers, 11, Lubo Ivanko, 16, richjem, 7, THEPALMER, 5, VisualCommunications, 17; Shutterstock: Art Konovalov, 15, Krysja, 9, MakDill, 10, Marc Bruxelle, 6, maxfluor, 14, Nik Merkulov, 21 (top), Petr Basel, 4, Pi-Lens, cover, back cover, Ryan King Art (background), throughout, xpixel, 21 (bottom)

Editorial Credits
Editor: Amy McDonald Maranville; Designer: Cynthia Della-Rovere; Media Researcher: Eric Gohl; Production Specialist: Katy LaVigne

All internet sites appearing in back matter were available and accurate when this book was sent to press.

Table of Contents

What Snowplows Do 4

Look Inside. 8

Look Outside. 12

    Snowplow Diagram 18

    Testing Snowplow Blades . . . 20

    Glossary 22

    Read More 23

    Internet Sites 23

    Index 24

Words in **bold** are in the glossary.

What Snowplows Do

Brrrr! It's cold outside. The snow is falling fast. Soon a thick layer of snow covers the roads. How will cars get through?

Here comes a snowplow! It has a **blade** at the front. It pushes the snow aside as it drives down the road. Soon the road is clear.

Many snowplows are big and powerful. Others are smaller. They can clear sidewalks or bike paths.

Some snowplows just clear snow. Others spread salt or sand on the roads as they drive. Salt helps melt snow and ice. Sand makes the roads less slippery.

Look Inside

The driver sits in the **cab**. It is at the front of the snowplow. The controls are inside. A switch or button turns on extra-bright lights. They help the driver see. The driver can also turn on flashing **warning** lights. A lever makes the blade go up and down.

The back of this snowplow has a spreader. It can spread sand or salt. Some snowplows use a mixture of both.

Sand or salt is poured into a **hopper**. There is a **chute** at the back. Salt or sand comes down the chute. The chute swings from side to side. It shoots out salt or sand. It covers the road evenly.

Look Outside

 A snowplow has a blade. It is at the front. Its bottom edge scrapes the road. Most blades are curved. Others are V-shaped. These can push through big snowbanks.

The blade is usually angled too. One end is farther forward. The other is farther back. This pushes the snow to one side of the road.

Snow and ice are slippery. They are hard to drive on. Some snowplows have tires with special **tread**. They help grip the road. Some snowplows even have chains on their tires for better grip.

Snow tires have big gaps in the tread. Some snow tires even have spikes. They stick out from the tire. They grip ice or packed snow.

Snow can fall at any time. Drivers often work at night. They also work in **blizzards**. It is hard to see in heavy snow. A snowplow has flashing warning lights. The lights are often yellow. They make it easy for other drivers to see the snowplow.

Snowplow Diagram

lights

blade

Testing Snowplow Blades

Snowplow blades are shaped differently. Test out how they work for yourself!

Make a pile of "snow." You can use sand, gravel, or crushed ice. Use cardboard to make a V-shaped blade and a curved blade. Push each one into your pile. Which blade moves the snow the easiest? Do the blades move the snow differently?

Glossary

blade (BLAYD)—the wide part of a snowplow that pushes the snow

blizzard (BLIZ-urd)—a storm with heavy snow and strong winds

cab (KAB)—the compartment at the front of a vehicle where the driver sits

chute (SHOOT)—a sloping passage or slide for moving things to a lower level

hopper (HOP-ur)—the part of a snowplow where salt or sand is loaded

tread (TRED)—a series of bumps and deep grooves on a tire

warning (WORN-ing)—something that tells others about something dangerous

Read More

Abbot, Henry. *I Want to Drive a Snowplow*. New York: PowerKids Press, 2017.

Arnold, Quinn M. *Snowplows*. Mankato, MN: Creative Education, 2019.

Meister, Cari. *Snowplows*. Minneapolis, MN: Bullfrog Books, 2016.

Internet Sites

Kids' Crossing: How Do Blizzards Form?
eo.ucar.edu/kids/dangerwx/blizzard3.htm

Truck Tunes: Snowplow
www.youtube.com/watch?v=5oa8P3HJhYw

Wonderopolis: Why Is Sand or Salt Put on Roads When it Snows?
www.wonderopolis.org/wonder/why-is-sand-or-salt-spread-on-the-road-when-it-snows

Index

bike paths, 6
blades, 5, 8, 12–13
blizzards, 16

cabs, 8
chains, 14
chutes, 11
controls, 8

hoppers, 11

ice, 7, 14, 15

lights, 8, 16

salt, 7, 10, 11
sand, 7, 10, 11
sidewalks, 6
spikes, 15
spreaders, 10

tires, 14–15
tread, 14–15